This book is dedicated to Four State Christian School—a place for learning and love.

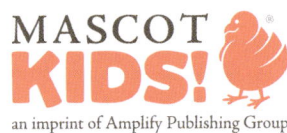

www.mascotbooks.com

Charlotte Shares Her Feelings

©2023 David Wermuth, LCSW. All Rights Reserved. No part of this publication may be reproduced, stored in a retrieval system or transmitted in any form by any means electronic, mechanical, or photocopying, recording or otherwise without the permission of the author.

For more information, please contact:
Mascot Kids, an imprint of Amplify Publishing Group
620 Herndon Parkway, Suite 220
Herndon, VA 20170
info@mascotbooks.com

Library of Congress Control Number: 2023904215

CPSIA Code: PRKF0423A
ISBN-13: 978-1-63755-803-4

Printed in China

CHARLOTTE
Shares Her Feelings

By David Wermuth, LCSW

Illustrated by Tamás Erdődi

Charlotte was a small mouse,
a little mouse indeed.

Smaller than adult mice,
so a big voice she would need.

And to the count of three,
Charlotte would speak,
to share what she felt to be…

"I'm scared, I'm scared, I'm scared!"
Charlotte shook as she yelped.

Charlotte feared the big stage,
thank God her two friends had helped.

And to the count of three,
Charlotte would speak,
to share what she felt to be…

"I'm glad, I'm glad, I'm glad," Charlotte shouted with glee.

Charlotte loved apple pie,
and a big slice she would see.

And to the count of three,
Charlotte would speak,
to share what she felt to be…

"I'm sad, I'm sad, I'm sad,"
Charlotte cried in her grief.

Charlotte lost her pet bug,
and a warm hug brought relief.

And to the count of three,
Charlotte would speak,
to share what she felt to be…

"I'm mad, I'm mad, I'm mad," Charlotte yelled with anger.

Charlotte hated taking baths,
yet her mom always made her.

And to the count of three,
Charlotte would speak,
to share what she felt to be…

"I'm bored, I'm bored, I'm bored," Charlotte whispered loudly.

Charlotte loathed her bedtime,
more playtime she needed so badly.

And to the count of three,
Charlotte would speak,
to share what she felt to be…

"I'm loved, I'm loved, I'm loved," Charlotte roared wholeheartedly.

Charlotte's love tank was filled,
filled by her whole family.

Charlotte had her own feelings,
feelings she could share with others.
You, too, can share your feelings,
so share them with one another.

THE END

QUESTIONS FOR EVERYONE TO ANSWER!

Easy Questions:

When did you feel bored today?

_____

When did you feel mad today?

_____

When did you feel happy today?

_____

When did you feel sad today?

_____

Hard Questions:

When was the last time you cried?

___

When was the last time you were hugged?

___

When was the last time you felt scared?

___

When was the last time you felt brave?

___

About the Author

David Wermuth, LCSW is a licensed therapist in Southwest Missouri. He specializes in working with children and families, and has gained experiences from being a preschool teacher, youth pastor, foster parent, and mental health therapist. David enjoys cooking, traveling, and spending time with family.